W9-DAS-363

MONEY TROUBLE

The Corner Kids

Written by Larry Dane Brimner • Illustrated by Christine Tripp

SCHOLASTIC INC.

New York   Toronto   London   Auckland   Sydney
Mexico City   New Delhi   Hong Kong   Buenos Aires

For Lee Bennett Hopkins
—L.D.B.

For my daughter Elizabeth
—C.T.

Reading Consultants

Linda Cornwell
Coordinator of School Quality and Professional Improvement
(Indiana State Teachers Association)

Katharine A. Kane
Education Consultant
(Retired, San Diego County Office of Education and San Diego State University)

No part of this publication may be reproduced in whole or in part, or stored in a retrieval system, or transmitted in any form or by any means, electronic, mechanical, photocopying, recording, or otherwise, without written permission of the publisher. For information regarding permission, write to Permissions Department, Grolier Incorporated, a subsidiary of Scholastic Inc., 90 Old Sherman Turnpike, Danbury, CT 06816.

ISBN 0-516-24130-3

Copyright © 2001 by Larry Dane Brimner. Illustrations copyright © 2001 by Christine Tripp. All rights reserved. Published by Scholastic Inc., 557 Broadway, New York, NY 10012. SCHOLASTIC and associated logos are trademarks and/or registered trademarks of Scholastic Inc.

12 11 10 9 8 7 6 5   7/0

Printed in China.   62

First Scholastic printing, March 2002

This book is about
responsibility.

"I'm leaving for the library, Mom,"
Alex said.

"Don't forget to pick up milk on the way home," his mother said. She tucked a five dollar bill into his pocket.

Alex dashed out the door.

Alex met up with his friends
Gabby and Three J at
the library. They called
themselves the Corner Kids.

"Let's find seats," said
Three J. "We don't want
to miss the show."

"I'll catch up," said Alex.
"I want to get a book."

In no time, Alex was back.
"I can't wait to read this!" he said.

"Shhh!" said Gabby.
"The show is starting."

Alex marked his place.

A clown in a fuzzy
orange wig said,
"Introducing . . .
Amazing Matilda!"
A little white dog
sprang out of a box.

After the show, the Corner Kids
stopped at Two Sisters' Market.

Alex put the milk on the counter.
He reached in his pocket.

"The money," he said.
"It's gone!"

"Are you sure?" asked Three J.

"Check your pockets," said Gabby.

"Maybe you dropped it," said Three J.

"Maybe," said Alex.

The Corner Kids looked everywhere.

Later, Alex sighed.
"I guess I better go," he said.

Alex tried to sneak in,
but the door squeaked. *Squeak!*

"Hi, Alex!" His mother smiled.
"Did you remember the milk?"

"Yes," Alex said. It wasn't really a lie.
He had *remembered*, but saying
it made his stomach feel bumpy.

"Then where is it?" she asked.
Alex bit his bottom lip.

"Alex?" said his mother.

"Somebody took the money," he said.

"Are you sure?" his mother asked.

Alex thought. He thought some more.
Then he remembered something.

Alex opened his book.
He found the money!

"I thought I lost it," he said.
"I was afraid you would get mad."

"Perhaps," his mother said.
"But we can only solve problems
when we know the truth."
Alex nodded.

"I know a way to solve this problem,"
his mother said.

They walked to Two Sisters' Market together.

TWO
SISTERS'
MARKET

STOP

ABOUT THE AUTHOR

Larry Dane Brimner studied literature and writing at San Diego State University and taught school for twenty years. The author of more than seventy-five books for children, many of them Children's Press titles, he enjoys meeting young readers and writers when he isn't at his computer.

ABOUT THE ILLUSTRATOR

Christine Tripp lives in Ottawa, Canada, with her husband Don; four grown children—Elizabeth, Erin, Emily, and Eric; son-in-law Jason; grandsons Brandon and Kobe; four cats; and one very large, scruffy puppy named Jake.

Rookie choices®

Meet the Corner Kids—Alex, Three J, and Gabby. These spunky second graders are best friends who live in apartment buildings on the corner of the same street. No matter what the adventure, the Corner Kids are willing to listen to each other, make thoughtful choices, and learn from their mistakes.

Rookie Choices® is a series designed to encourage the development of good character. Each book focuses on an important decision-making trait or skill. As readers follow the Corner Kids through real-life situations, they will recognize the positive results of good choices. The engaging text and amusing illustrations make these books excellent supplements to character education materials.

Money Trouble promotes responsibility.

This edition is only available for distribution through the school market.

SCHOLASTIC INC.

0-516-24130-3